My Queen You Are!

Md. Ziaul Haque

ISBN: 9798634811482

DEDICATION

To the generous souls who are fighting so hard against the enemy-
CORONA VIRUS!

CONTENTS

My Queen You Are!

My Queen You Are!

My Queen You Are!

My Queen you are!

I am your King,

I have a kingdom,

The Kingdom of Love!

In my Kingdom of Love,

Celestial you will feel,

Like that of the actual heaven,

Believe me, I will keep my promise!

May I have the pleasure of taking you,

To the journey of love please?

I Care for Her

I care for her,

More than I care for myself,

Since she is my love,

She is my life!

I will continue to love her,

As long as the clock ticks,

In my body,

She makes me feel immortal!

As the moon is energized by the sun,

I feel like the same when she is around!

The Birds do not Sing Darling

Hey listen! Right there!

Sitting on the branch of the tree!

How sweetly the birds sing!

Can't you hear my dear?

Yes, I can but they aren't singing!

What? Yes, they are!

No, you must know one thing,

What should I know then?

The birds do not sing darling,

They talk to each other!

Iago: The Murderer

Iago = I am ego,

'I' 'a'm e'go'!

A Satan in the guise of a man,

A green-eyed monster!

Iago has used Othello as a weapon,

To murder Desdemona,

And disturbed the Moor so much that,

He leads himself towards self-destruction!

It is rather rational to say then,

It is none but Iago who 'is' the 'murderer'!

Flow

Flow like the stream of consciousness,

Let your beauty glow,

As the full moon,

Be love and be loved!

Let me fondle you,

As this is the wedding night,

Let us be one,

Let us be in paradise!

Only kisses and passionate love,

May find their places between you and me!

For the Sake of Intimacy

Intimate we were,

Like the two kissing roses,

Dreamy the days were,

Celestial was every moment!

Like the birds,

We used to communicate,

When the days were bright,

Like the diamonds and the nights young!

As the embrace of the galaxies,

Into each other we lost for eternity!

Buy-cycle!

Don't ever get confused please,

Seeing the title 'buy-cycle' instead of bicycle!

It's not a spelling mistake,

It's a sort of guidance you may say!

Buy cycle and start cycling,

Be on the move,

As the earth is around the sun!

A marvelous exercise cycling really is!

Rightly said by Albert Einstein - "Life is like riding a bicycle,

To keep your balance you must keep moving!"

Never get Brainwashed!

Control yourself!

Relax,

Read books,

Know thyself; know the world!

Create an invisible shield around you,

Protect yourself,

Don't let anyone harm you ever,

Both psychologically and physically!

Don't believe everything blindly,

Be reasonable and inquisitive ever!

Blue Whale Game

The one who leads you to commit suicide,

The one who is Satan but acts as a friend,

Is garbage himself!

A sinner from and to HELL!

Someone has created the game,

Not to destroy himself after playing it,

But to destroy the innocent ones,

Such is his unpardonable hypocrisy!

Every life on earth is special; no life is a waste!

Identify the satanic impulses and stay away NOW!

Empty Headed

Highly intelligent I thought she was,

Turned out upside down,

Just a person with an empty head,

Was she really was!

Made countless mistakes,

Over and over again,

Within a very short span of time,

With scarcely any lesson learnt!

May God bless her by the way!

May God show her the way out!

About the Author

Md. Ziaul Haque is originally from Zakiganj, Sylhet, Bangladesh. He is an award-winning poet, writer, actor, novelist, dramatist, director, film writer [screenwriter], literary critique, academic, thinker, philosopher, singer, songwriter, short story writer, rhymer, translator, reviewer, columnist, essayist, researcher and scholar. He earned his B.A [Hon's] and Master's degrees in English language and literature from Shah Jalal University of Science & Technology, Sylhet. His pen name is 'Shobdoraj' in Bangla and its translation is 'King of Words' in English. He is honourably called 'The Poet of Creativity' and 'The Great Poet' by the readers. Md. Ziaul Haque's writings are frequently published in the famous national and international literary journals, newspapers and magazines.

He invented many words, terms, literary and poetic forms: "Poetenry" [poems of ten lines], "Kurine" [poems of twenty lines], "Distant-author" [a writer who is currently a citizen of another country but writes about his motherland and its people, culture etc.], "Prosaic-ideas" [ideas in brain appear in prosaic forms, they do not normally follow any metrical composition], "Translation of Objects" [in literary works, objects can also be translated and mistranslated since they are considered as equivalents to something else], "Post-postmodern Age" [the proposed name of the era after Postmodernism as the writer mentioned in a newspaper article], "Intentional Delay of Vision" [not seeing or avoiding the reality intentionally], "Jealouty" [jealousy + beauty]- [a feeling of being jealous of another person's beauty or handsomeness; in Bangla, Porosrikatorota], "Inextrovert" [introvert + extrovert]- [a person who is normally quiet or shy and feels uneasy to talk to other people but sometimes becomes friendly and likes the company of others], "Kidultnap" [kid + adult + nap]- [the action of taking away both kids and adults by force to detain them as prisoners and demand money from their family members for returning them], "Foolligent" [fool + intelligent]- [a person who behaves foolishly sometimes but acts intelligently in certain circumstances; foolish but sometimes intelligent], defined the word "Simplex" in a new way- [Simple + Complex = Simplex]- [A problem or something else that seems simple but is complex actually], "A Writer's Religious Partiality" [A writer's religious partiality becomes clear when he chooses the names of the characters for most of his stories, novels etc. from his own religion], "Prosetic" [Prosaic + Poetic]- [A poem that is prosaic in form but looks poetic also since it has rhymes], "Consequential Colonialism" [The names of places of the colonised countries that remind the local citizens about the colonial moments of the past], "Smellwitness" [A person who has smelt something and is able to tell about it to others], "Poeten"- [The poet who writes only ten-line-poems], "Poestory" [Poetry + Story]- [A new genre of writing in literature that is created by blending two words i.e. poetry + story. In a word, it is a type of writing where a story has both the qualities of poetry and prose; in Bangla- Golpita], "Prosetry" [Prose + Poetry]- [Having the qualities of both prose and poetry], "Death-vision in the Objects and Minor Accidents"- [Objects and minor accidents that sometimes indicate at bigger and terrible accidents where people may die], "Haqueian Verse" [A new form of poetry created by me is called 'Haqueian Verse', which starts with a single word; it has five lines that contain ten words in total. The poem ends with a single word that rhymes with the first word], "Murder Committed by Using Words and Gestures" [Iago drives Othello towards the point of insanity by spreading rumour about Desdemona. He suffers psychologically as his honour is at a stake and his self-respect is ruined. As a result, Othello murders his wife; Broadly, Iago commits the murder of Desdemona and Othello by using his cunning words and gestures.],

"Deathreat" or "Dethreat" [An expression of intention to murder someone; a threat by one person or a group of people to kill another person or group of people.], "Philogy" [Philogy is a mixture of two words- Philosophy and Logic. It means the study of philosophy and logic at the same time. In other words, it is the branch of knowledge that deals with philosophy and logic.], "Philogical" [Philogical is a mixture of two words- Philosophical and Logical. It means an idea, expression or thought that is philosophical and logical at the same time.], "Medition" [Medition is a noun and verb. It is a mixture of two words- Medicine + Meditation. As a noun, it means the action or practice of meditating or meditioning by taking some friendly medicines or drugs that have no side-affects. It is the act of taking some legal or less harmful drugs and giving one's attention to only one thing as a way of becoming calm and relaxed. However, the drugs are not allowed in the religious meditations; as a verb, it means to take harmless drugs and think deeply about something. It also means to take drugs that have no side-affects and think calm thoughts in order to relax. However, drugs are not allowed in religious kinds of meditations.], "Shakespeareius" [It is a noun and adjective; a mixture of two words- Shakespeare + Genius. As a noun, it means someone who has William Shakespeare's exceptional, intellectual or creative power in him; as an adjective, it means a person, ideas, writings, thoughts etc. have the qualities or characteristics of William Shakespeare or his writings], "Fiverse" [Five + Verse: Poems of Five Lines, a new poetic form created or invented by me. In Bangla, it is called Panchpodee Kobita. There are 5 lines and total 15 words in it. 1st line has 1 word; 2nd line has 2 words; 3rd line has 3 words; 4th line has 4 words and 5th line has 5 words. 1st line rhymes with the 2nd line; 3rd line is unrhymed; 4th and 5th lines rhyme with each other. The rhyme scheme is: AABCC. There are no punctuation marks at the end of the lines], "Powery" ['Powery' is an adjective that is similar to 'powerful'. It means having great power or strength.], "Songer" [A songer is a person who writes songs or lyrics. It also means a person who writes popular songs or the music for them.], "Tennet" [Poems of Ten Lines], "Ellian" [The teachers, students, researchers, things etc. of English Language and Literature (ELL)], "Chattogramian" [A person from Chattogram, which is a port-city in Bangladesh. Belonging to or relating to

Chattogram or its people. The city was previously called Chittagong.], "Sporshophone" [That is what he calls the 'Touch Phone' in Bangla]. His favourite pastime activities include- playing chess, listening to good music, angling and occasional theatre directing. In addition, he likes to keep in touch with the friends and readers on the various social networking sites. His writings are full of 'creativity'. It is worth mentioning that he is a dreamer and optimistic by nature. He dreams of making films! At present, he teaches English Language and Literature at University of Creative Technology, Chittagong, Bangladesh.

List of His Books

Language/Translation:

1. Advanced Reading and Writing, The Easy Way [2011]

2. Advanced Reading and Writing: History, Developments, Concepts and Techniques [2014]

3. Prose Translation: Problems and Solutions [2017]

Poetry/Poetenry/Kurine/Epic/Haqueian Verse/Fiverse-

1. Give Me a Sky to Fly [2014]

2. Fragrance of Love [2014]

3. Hazrat Shah Jalal (R.A): Ekti Mohakabbo [Hazrat Shah Jalal (R.A): An Epic] [2015]

4. Poems of Love [2015]

5. Poetenry: Poems of Ten Lines [2015]

6. Kurine: Poems of Twenty Lines [2015]

7. A Farewell to Love [2016]

8. Do not 'FALL' in Love, 'RISE' in Love! [2017]

9. Haqueian Verse: A New Poetic Form [2017]

10. Fiverse: Poems of Five Lines [2018]

11. Sexual Poetenry: Poems of Ten Lines [2019]

12. Sexual Fiverse: Poems of Five Lines [2019]

13. Tennet: Poems of Ten Lines [2019]

14. Erotic Fiverse: Poems of Five Lines [2019]

15. LUV All Around [2019]

16. The Last Embrace! [2019]

17. The New Literary & Poetic Forms Created by Md. Ziaul Haque [2020]

18. A Wall of Love [2020]

19. Be the Sky! [2020]

20. Let the Universe Know [2020]

21. A New Tide of Love [2020]

Religion:

1. Eastern Thoughts Islam, Hinduism, Buddhism and Beyond [2015]

Religion and Science/Philosophy:

1. Visions and Deaths: Trying to Reveal the Mystery behind the Extremely Unnatural Deaths [2016]

Short Story:

1. Hell Followed Him! [2015]

2. Characterless [2015]

3. Kivabe Manuske Pagol Banano Hoy? [How are the People Driven Mad?] [2019]

Literary Criticism:

1. The Shakespeare-mystery: Much Ado about Nothing [2015]

2. Othello's Murder [not suicide] by Iago! [2017]

Children:

1. Rocket in My Pocket [2015]

2. Tom and Jerry [2016]

3. Rat in the Hat [2016]

4. Voyonkor Sublet [Scary Sublet] [2016]

5. Pokemon [2017]

6. Batman [2018]

Songs/Lyrics:

1. Love Songs of Md. Ziaul Haque [2016]

Poestory [Poetry + Story]:

1. Poestory [Poetry + Story]: A New Literary Form Created by Md. Ziaul Haque [2017]

Essay/Article:

1. Not English, We Want a New International Language! [2018]

Quotes:

1. Famous Quotes of Md. Ziaul Haque [2020]

Get in Touch with Md. Ziaul Haque

E-mail: zia@uctc.edu.bd

mdziaulhaque708@gmail.com

Twitter: https://twitter.com/mdziaulhaque83

Facebook: https://www.facebook.com/zhaque1

Facebook Fan Page: https://www.facebook.com/mdziaulhaque2014

Amazon: https://www.amazon.com/Md.-Ziaul-Haque/e/B00KENUD7S%3Fref=dbs_a_mng_rwt_scns_share